Lila and the Swallows

Written by
Qi Zhi

Illustrated by
Cheng Yue

CARDINAL
MEDIA

It was spring and the swallows flew back from the south.

They flew over rivers.

They flew
between
willows.

They flew through the clouds.

Lila ran outside
to welcome them.
"Hello, swallows!" she said.

The swallows circled three times over her head.

Then they flew to their nest
that was still on the beam
in Lila's courtyard.

"I am glad to see you return," Lila said.

In the summer, Lila and the swallows caught bugs together.

Lila imagined what it would
be like to fly with them.

They could fly near corn fields.

They could fly
past cotton
fields.

They could fly over water lilies.

But summer passed and
the air became cold.

Lila saw some wild geese flying south.

She knew the swallows
were preparing to leave.

Lila imagined flying south in the autumn sky with her swallow friends.

She wished them a safe journey.
"See you again in the spring!"